A MESSAGE TO PARENTS

It is of vital importance for parents to read good books to young children in order to aid the child's psychological and intellectual development. At the same time as stimulating the child's imagination and awareness of his environment, it creates a positive relationship between parent and child. The child will gradually increase his basic vocabulary and will soon be able to read books alone.

Brown Watson has published this series of books with these aims in mind. By collecting this inexpensive library, parent and child are provided with hours of pleasurable and profitable reading.

Katie
and the Carnival

Text by Maureen Spurgeon

Brown Watson
ENGLAND

Katie loved Carnival Week!

Fairy lights and decorations hung everywhere, with the whole of Honeyridge looking forward to the fancy dress races around the streets, singing and dancing in the Town Centre, pet shows, a fun fair, and – best of all – the Carnival Parade along the High Street!

"I thought we'd have a float, this year!" smiled Miss Croft, Katie's Play School Teacher. "What's a float?" asked Katie.

"It's what you ride on for the Carnival Parade!" said Doreen Maggs.

"My cousin Glenda is the Carnival Queen," she went on, "so I'm going to be Carnival Princess! I've got a dress that reaches right down to my ankles, AND I'm having a cloak AND a crown!"

Katie tried hard not to listen. Nobody liked Doreen much — mostly because she was just always telling everyone what she thought they hadn't done, what they ought to do, and how she could do it better!

Soon, Miss Croft was showing them how to crumple lots of newspapers to make enough flowers to turn Mr. Pegg's trailer into the Play School carnival float! "When we paint them," she said, "they'll look really nice!"

Only Doreen Maggs did not join in.

"We're having bigger flowers than those on the Carnival Queen's float!" she kept saying. "AND lots of shiny streamers! AND great, big balloons!"

"It sounds lovely, Doreen!" smiled Miss Croft. Then, she sighed. "It's a shame we can't have something like that on our float – something to make sure everyone notices us in the parade."

They had all been working so hard, nobody noticed it was time to go home.

Miss Croft was pleased when both Katie's Daddy and Darren's Daddy, Mr. Wood, stayed to help with the tidying-up!

And still the talk went on about the Carnival and the Play School float!

"I could let you have a bouncy castle," suggested Mr. Wood. "Then Katie and her friends can bounce all through the parade!"

It sounded a lovely idea!

"That would make our float look really special," smiled Miss Croft. "If you're sure it's no trouble...."

"No trouble at all!" said Mr. Wood. "I will bring it along, myself!"

All that week, Katie and her friends made lots and lots of paper flowers. Then on the evening before the parade, Mr. Pegg brought his truck and trailer round to the back of the Play School Hall.

Miss Croft showed them how to thread the flowers on to string to make the garlands which would hang all around the truck and trailer. Katie couldn't wait to see the bouncy castle in the middle!

The next day, Katie's Mummy helped her to get ready, and they set off for the Town Centre. Lots of people were there already, waiting for the parade to begin.

"There's Mr. Wood!" shouted Katie. "Look, Mummy! He's got our bouncy castle!"

She could see Darren and Suzy helping Mr. Wood to blow the castle up.

"A bit more air inside," puffed Mr. Wood, "then we'll load the castle on to the float. We can finish pumping it up, once it's in place! Grab a rope and help me please, Katie!"

What happened next, nobody quite knew. Either Mr. Wood's pumping machine started to go wrong, or someone let go of one of the ropes, or there was a sudden gust of wind.....

But the bouncy castle lifted itself off the ground and began rising up into the air!

"Hold tight, Katie!" cried Mr. Wood, scrambling towards her. "Don't let go of the rope!"

"What is all the shouting about?" came another voice, some-one they all knew. "I thought you were all coming to see the Carnival Queen's float before we start leading the parade to the park!"

Then, Doreen Maggs looked up and saw the bottom of the bouncy castle, stuck in a tree.

"Where did you get that giant balloon?" she screamed. "Our float is the one that ought to have giant balloons!"

Next minute, she had snatched
the rope from Katie's hand!

"Now, you know-------" she
began, her voice becoming a
high-pitched wail, as both her
feet left the ground at once!
Everybody started laughing!

"Help! Help!" screamed Doreen.
"Help, somebody! I – I'm floating
away!"

Miss Croft and Mr. Wood tried
to get the rope and pull her
down, but it was just out of their
reach!

"Aaaagh!" screamed Doreen Maggs. "Aaagh! I want to come down!" There was a jerk, and Doreen floated up a few more inches! Then – BANG! A sharp twig had made a hole in the bouncy castle!

The bang made Doreen let go of the rope. She fell into Mr. Pegg's trailer!

"Ow-ow!" she shouted. "I-I'm hurt!"

"What?" laughed Mr. Pegg. "When you and the bouncy castle came down together?"

"I – I've got to go back to the Carnival Queen!" she wailed, looking down at her dirty dress and shoes.

"She's already leading the parade!" said someone in the crowd. "You'd best go on the Play School float."